GOBLIN

by Sue Fliess
illustrated by Piper Thibodeau

Grosset & Dunlap
An Imprint of Penguin Random House

For Elfi and Maurice, who
love and protect nature—SF
To my favorite art teacher,
Renate Heidersdorf—PT

GROSSET & DUNLAP
Penguin Young Readers Group
An Imprint of Penguin Random House LLC

Text copyright © 2016 by Sue Fliess. Illustrations copyright © 2016 by Penguin Random House LLC.
All rights reserved. Published by Grosset & Dunlap, an imprint of Penguin Random House LLC,
345 Hudson Street, New York, New York 10014. GROSSET & DUNLAP is a trademark of
Penguin Random House LLC. Manufactured in China.

Library of Congress Cataloging-in-Publication Data is available.

ISBN 9780448489339   10 9 8 7 6 5 4 3

In the forest of Scarewood, where gremlins made sweets,
a creature named Goblin Hood guarded their treats.

They worked all year long—
one big candy machine—
to make scrumptious sweets for the next Halloween.

One Halloween Eve when the candy was done,
and the gremlins were wrapping up every last one . . .

a witch who loved candy was soaring nearby
and decided she'd steal all their candy and fly.

She swooped in and cast a dark spell on the wood—
turning the gremlins against Goblin Hood!

Under her curse, they were forced to obey.

As they stacked all the candy,
she took it away.

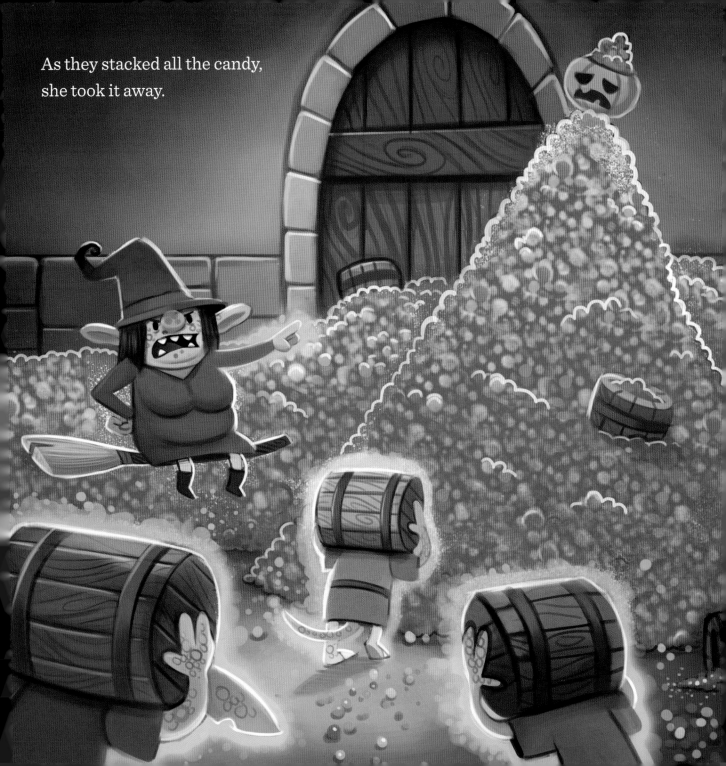

No candy was spared—that mean witch took it all.
Marshmallows! Truffles! The big and the small.
The toffees and candy bars, brittles and pops.
The licorice, gummies, and lemony drops!

She bagged up the treats from the factory room.
"You gremlins will load it all onto my broom!"

Goblin Hood knew that he had to act fast
to take back the treats before Halloween passed.

He worked out a plan where he would not be seen.
He'd fight off the witch and he'd save Halloween.

Using the candy he'd stashed in his pack,

he climbed up the walls
and he snuck in the back.

He lassoed the witch with his licorice strands.
"We're done with your curses and evil demands!"

Stretching some taffy, he bound up her feet

and glued her with bubble gum right to her seat.

"I'm taking your wand, and you're going away."

"But please," begged the witch, "all I want is to stay."

"I just wanted sweets.
From now on I'll be good.
I'll never again cast a spell
on this wood."

"You'll have to make up for the things you did wrong.

And help make the Halloween treats all year long."

So Goblin Hood gave her a job in the shop:

to carefully push every stick in each pop.

Meanwhile, the young trick-or-treaters had come, hoping for jelly beans, chocolate, and gum.

With plenty of candy and no more to fear,
the gremlins of Scarewood all let out a cheer.
"The spell has been broken, and everything's right.
Our great Goblin Hood has saved Halloween night!"

Goblin Hood and the gremlins of Scarewood
are getting ready for Halloween. But when a
witch takes all their candy, it's up to Goblin Hood
to steal from the witch and give to the poor
little gremlins!

GROSSET&DUNLAP
www.penguin.com/youngreaders

ISBN 978-0-448-48933-9

EAN

9 780448 489339

50399>